D1221197

That's What Friends Are For

That's What Friends Are For

by **FLORENCE PARRY HEIDE** and **SYLVIA WORTH VAN CLIEF**

Pictures by BRINTON TURKLE

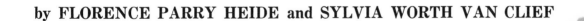

FOUR WINDS PRESS · NEW YORK

Second printing, 1970

Published by Four Winds Press
A Division of Scholastic Magazines, Inc., New York, N. Y.
Text copyright © 1968 by Florence Parry Heide and
Sylvia Worth Van Clief. Illustrations copyright
© 1968 by Brinton Turkle.
Library of Congress Catalogue Card Number: 68-27267

Theodore, the elephant,
is sitting in the middle of the forest.
He has hurt his leg.

What a pity!
Today Theodore was going
to meet his cousin
at the end of the forest.

"What can I do?" Theodore says.
"My cousin is at the end of the forest,
and here I am in the middle of the forest.
And I have a bad leg, and I can't walk."

"I know what I'll do," Theodore says.
"I'll ask my friends for advice.
That's what friends are for."

Along comes Theodore's friend, the bird.

"Why are you sitting here
in the middle of the forest?"
asks the bird.

"Because I have a bad leg,
and I can't walk.
And I can't meet my cousin
at the end of the forest," says Theodore.

"If *I* had a bad leg,
I would fly to the end of the forest,"
says the bird to Theodore.

"It's nice of you to give advice,"
says Theodore to the bird.

"That's what friends are for,"
says the bird.

Along comes Theodore's friend,
the daddy-long-legs.

"Why are you sitting here
in the middle of the forest?"
asks the daddy-long-legs.

"Because I have a bad leg,
and I can't walk.
And I can't fly.
And I can't meet my cousin
at the end of the forest," says Theodore.

"If *I* had a bad leg,"
says the daddy-long-legs,
"I could walk anyhow —
because I have seven other legs."

"It's nice of you to give advice,"
says Theodore.

"That's what friends are for,"
says the daddy-long-legs.

Along comes Theodore's friend, the monkey.

"Why are you sitting here
in the middle of the forest?"
asks the monkey.

"Because I have a bad leg,
and I can't walk.
And I can't fly.
And I don't have seven other legs.
And I can't meet my cousin
at the end of the forest," says Theodore.

"If *I* had a bad leg," says the monkey,
"I would swing by my tail from the trees,
like this."

"Well," says Theodore,
"I may have a very weak *tail*,
but I have a very strong *trunk*."

Theodore grabs a branch of the tree
with his trunk...

Crash!

"Well, anyhow," says Theodore,
"thank you for your advice."

"That's what friends are for,"
says the monkey.

Along comes Theodore's friend, the crab.

"Why are you lying down
in the middle of the forest?"
asks the crab.

"Because I have a bad leg,
and I can't walk.
And I can't fly.
And I don't have seven other legs.
And I can't swing from the trees
by my tail (OR my trunk).
And I can't meet my cousin
at the end of the forest," says Theodore.

"If *I* had a bad leg," says the crab,
"I would get rid of it and
grow another one."

"It's nice of you to give advice,"
says Theodore.

"That's what friends are for,"
says the crab.

Along comes Theodore's friend, the lion.

"Why are you sitting here
in the middle of the forest?"
asks the lion.

"Because I have a bad leg,
and I can't walk.
And I can't fly.
And I don't have seven other legs.
And I can't swing from the trees
by my tail (OR my trunk).
And I can't grow another leg.
And I can't meet my cousin
at the end of the forest," says Theodore.

"If *I* had a bad leg," says the lion,
"I would roar so loud
that everyone in the whole forest
would hear me, and come running
to see what was the matter."

And he roars.

"What's all the noise?"
the opossum asks.
He is hanging upside down by his tail.

Theodore's friends
all begin to talk at once.
"Theodore can't fly,"
says the bird.

"He can't get to the end of the forest
to see his cousin," says the lion.
"We are giving him advice.
That's what friends are for."

"Nonsense," says the opossum.
"Friends are to *help*.
Bring the cousin to *Theodore*."

So all the friends
go to find Theodore's cousin
at the end of the forest.

And they bring the cousin
to Theodore.

Theodore and the cousin
and all the friends are having a party.

"Thank you for *helping* me,"
says Theodore to his friends.

"That's what friends are for,"
say the friends.

To give advice is very nice,
but friends can do much more.
Friends should always help a friend.
That's what friends are for!